BARRY LOPEZ

Light Action in the Caribbean

Barry Lopez is the author of six works of nonfiction and eight works of fiction. His writing appears regularly in *Harper's*, *The Paris Review*, *DoubleTake*, and *The Georgia Review*. He is the recipient of a National Book Award, an Award in Literature from the American Academy of Arts and Letters, a Guggenheim Fellowship, and other honors. He lives in western Oregon.

ety. I'm wondering—could I ever send her out? Maybe to help? Would you spend a few days with her?"

"I'd be glad to speak with her," he said, after considering the question. "I'd train her, if it came to that."

"Thank you."

He began squaring the maps up to place them back in the drawer.

"You know, Mister Trevino—Phillip, if I may, and you may call me Corlis—the question is about you, really." He shut the drawer and gestured me toward the door of the room, which he closed behind us.

"You represent a questing but lost generation of people. I think you know what I mean. You made it clear this morning, talking nostalgically about my books, that you think an elegant order has disappeared, something that shows the way." We were standing at the corner of the dining table with our hands on the chair backs. "It's wonderful, of course, that you brought your daughter into our conversation tonight, and certainly we're both going to have to depend on her, on her thinking. But the real question, now, is what will *you* do? Because you can't expect her to take up something you wish for yourself, a way of seeing the world. You send her here, if it turns out to be what she wants, but don't make the mistake of thinking you, or I or anyone, knows how the world is meant to work. The world is a miracle, unfolding in the pitch dark. We're lighting candles. Those maps—they are my candles. And I can't extinguish them for anyone."

He crossed to his shelves and took down his copy of *The City of Geraniums*. He handed it to me and we went to the door.

"If you want to come back in the morning for breakfast, please do. Or, there is a cafe, the Dogwood, next to the motel. It's good. However you wish."

We said good night and I moved out through pools of dark beneath the ash trees to where I'd parked the car. I set the book on the seat opposite and started the engine. The headlights swept the front of the house as I turned past it, catching the salute of his hand, and then he was gone.

I inverted the image of the map from his letter in my mind and began driving south to the highway. After a few moments I turned off the headlights and rolled down the window. I listened to the tires crushing gravel in the roadbed. The sound of it helped me hold the road, together with instinct and the memory of earlier having driven it. I felt the volume of space beneath the clear, star-ridden sky, and moved over the dark prairie like a barn-bound horse.

ALSO BY BARRY LOPEZ

ABOUT THIS LIFE

In *About This Life*, Barry Lopez turns, for the first time, to autobiographical reflections. Whether traveling to Antarctica or Bonaire, Hokkaido or the Galápagos, or remembering the California and New York of his childhood, Lopez probes the mysterious connections among landscape, memory, and imagination.

Literature/Nature/0-679-75447-4

ARCTIC DREAMS

Arctic Dreams, a National Book Award winner for nonfiction, is an unforgettable study of the Far North, the hauntingly pure land of stunted forests and frozen seas, of muskox and narwhal. Barry Lopez offers a stunning compendium of biology, anthropology, and history in this jubilant examination of the Arctic terrain and wildlife.

Natural History/0-375-72748-5

THE REDISCOVERY OF NORTH AMERICA

Five hundred years ago, Christopher Columbus came to America and began a process not of discovery but of incursion—a "ruthless, angry search for wealth"—that continues today. This provocative book draws a direct line between the atrocities of the Spanish conquistadors and the ongoing pillage of our lands and waters, and challenges us to adopt an ethic that will make further depredations impossible.

Natural History/0-679-74099-6

WINTER COUNT

In these resonant and unpredictable stories Barry Lopez uses a few deft strokes to produce painfully beautiful scenes: a flock of great blue herons descends through a snowstorm to the streets of New York; a ghostly herd of buffalo sings a song of death. Combining the real with the wondrous, he presents a vision of people alive to the immediacy and spiritual truth of nature.

Fiction/Short Stories/0-679-78141-2

Also available: *Crossing Open Ground*, 0-679-72183-5

VINTAGE BOOKS
Available at your local bookstore, or call toll-free to order:
1-800-793-2665 (credit cards only).